Dear Parent:
Your child's love of r

Every child learns to read in a different way and at his or her own speed. Some go back and forth between reading levels and read favorite books again and again. Others read through each level in order. You can help your young reader improve and become more confident by encouraging his or her own interests and abilities. From books your child reads with you to the first books he or she reads alone, there are I Can Read Books for every stage of reading:

SHARED READING
Basic language, word repetition, and whimsical illustrations, ideal for sharing with your emergent reader

BEGINNING READING
Short sentences, familiar words, and simple concepts for children eager to read on their own

READING WITH HELP
Engaging stories, longer sentences, and language play for developing readers

READING ALONE
Complex plots, challenging vocabulary, and high-interest topics for the independent reader

ADVANCED READING
Short paragraphs, chapters, and exciting themes for the perfect bridge to chapter books

I Can Read Books have introduced children to the joy of reading since 1957. Featuring award-winning authors and illustrators and a fabulous cast of beloved characters, I Can Read Books set the standard for beginning readers.

A lifetime of discovery begins with the magical words **"I Can Read!"**

Visit www.icanread.com for information
on enriching your child's reading experience.

Marley & Me

Meet Marley

Adapted by Natalie Engel

Based on the screenplay written by Scott Frank and Don Roos

Based on the book *Marley & Me: Life and Love with the World's Worst Dog*
by John Grogan published by William Morrow,
an imprint of HarperCollins Publishers in 2005.

HarperCollins®, ☰®, and I Can Read Book® are trademarks of HarperCollins Publishers.

Library of Congress catalog card number: 2008933160
ISBN 978-0-06-170439-0

❖

First Edition

Marley & Me
Meet Marley

HarperCollins*Publishers*

Meet Marley.

Marley is a playful puppy

who loves to make new friends.

He loves to play new games.

Marley is a dog

with lots of zip.

When Marley was born,

he was the smallest puppy

in his litter.

But Jenny doesn't mind.

"I think this is the dog

for us," says Jenny.

John takes Marley home

for the first time.

"This is your house," he says.

Marley is excited

to have a family.

Marley loves his new home.

But sometimes,

he has trouble following the rules.

Marley runs on the beach

without his leash.

"Marley, no!" says John.

Marley makes a big mess

in the garage.

"Marley, no!" says Jenny.

One day,

Marley even steals a turkey

from the people next door.

"Marley, no!" says John.

"Sorry," Jenny tells

the people next door.

"Happy Thanksgiving."

John and Jenny know

that Marley tries to be good.

They hope Marley will stop being wild

when he grows up.

But as Marley grows bigger,

he wants to eat more.

Marley starts chewing

on everything he sees.

Marley chews on the couch.

Marley chews on the window blinds.

Then Marley chews

on Jenny's favorite things.

Jenny gets very angry.

"Bad dog!" yells Jenny.

"Why do you do this?

Why do you wreck everything?"

Jenny is upset.

She asks John

to take Marley for a walk.

So John and Marley

go to the beach.

John does some thinking.

Marley does some thinking, too.

When Marley and John come home,

Jenny is happy to see them.

She feels much better.

"I'm sorry," Jenny tells Marley.

"I may get mad,

but we are still family."

Jenny and Marley start to dance.

Marley feels very happy.

The next day,

John, Jenny, and Marley

go to the beach to play.

"Good boy!" says John.

"Good boy!" says Jenny.

"We love you," they say.

Marley loves them right back.

Marley is a very lucky dog.

He has a family who loves him.

Who could ask for more?